Maria Piórkowska-Urbania

The Adventures of Little Nenia

Nenia vs the Night Monsters

I don't know about you
but for me evenings
are the best time
of the day. Why?
Because everyone is at home,
and my unicorn backpack
is already full of things
for tomorrow,
the clothes are ironed
and it's time to play together.
This is my favourite part.

After supper mum takes Ludo out.
Then, while sipping tasty
cocoa, we play one game
before we go to sleep.
As usual, mum loses, while me
and dad take turns as winners.
We are pretty good at it. I comfort
mum, telling her
that one day she will
win as well.
Then mum says, "Unlucky at
cards, lucky in love,"
and winks at dad.

"Nenia, it's time for your bath, brush your teeth and go to bed, because we have to get up early tomorrow morning."

"Mummy, will you read to me just one chapter of 'The Mysterious Family of Fenicullids'?"

"I will, I will, now scoot to the bathroom" - she answers with a slight smile.

After the bath comes the ritual of reading, hugging, and tickling.

"Good night, Nenia... Sleep tight, don't let the bedbugs bite" - mum said, kissing me on the forehead.

"But if they do, then take your shoe" - I added.

"And beat them till they're black and blue!" - dad finished while standing in the doorway.
"I also want to give you a sweet kiss, one which will colour your dreams."
And so in all I received three kisses, and some bonus tickles. My dad is a Great Guy. That's what my mum always says, and I completely agree with her.

When my parents turned
off the light and shut the door, suddenly
the pipes started
to crunch, gurgle and screech.
Some strange shadows started dancing
on the wall and there
was a horrible, hairy monster
in the corner!
"Muuuum! Muuuum!"
"What happened, darling?!" - mum
asked, all scared.
"Mum, there is a horrible monster
in the corner!"
"Where?"
"It's right there, next to the door!"

Mum turned on the light, looked in the
corner and called dad, who was – as she
claimed – a real Slayer of Horrible Monsters
and would surely be able to help us get rid of it.
"What happened, Nenia? Did Casper visit you again?
We already established that he was a friendly ghost."
"No, dad! It was a completely
different, horrible monster."
"And can you describe it to us?
Then I can take my bookof monsters
and we can find a way to get rid of it.
You do remember that there is a way to deal with every
possible horrible monster there, right?"
"Yes, I remember, daddy. But I am so very scared of it..."
"I understand, Nenia, and if you describe
it to us, then we can help you."

"It stood in the corner, it was my height, it had no neck – its belly was connected to its head, it had very long, thin arms and legs.

It was all black and hairy. It had large, pointy ears, like a bat, small glowing eyes and a nose like a mole."

"You had a very good look for how dark the room is."

"Yes, too good" - as soon as I replied, I got really scared again, and I felt very hurt."

"So he looked kinda like the Jolly Devil, the one you saw in the movie?"

"Which one?" "The one which said: 'Me be silly, full of hair, me find rummage, me repair!' – we laughed about it so hard, remember?"

"I little bit, I guess."

"But he was a good devil, one who helped people."

"Now I know, it is the Raven Stench devil.
I'm sure you felt a smell
of something burning, right?"
"Yes, I did, but I thought it was the smell
of your burnt pancakes."
Mum snorted, and for a moment everyone
was cheerful but very soon dad
got all serious and returned to the topic.
"Alright, let's check if it is hiding somewhere."
We looked under the bed, behind
the curtains, under the table, behind
the dresser, and it was nowhere to be found.
Dad said that there were a few magical
ways to get rid of the unwanted guest.
He went to the kitchen and soon
returned with a small bottle.

"This is a magical mist which
clears the air, getting rid of all monsters.
All we need to do is spray the places where
the Raven Stench could be hiding, and he
will be gone for good."
And he did just that. But I still didn't feel
completely safe, I still had a feeling
that it may not be enough.
Seeing my doubt, mum brought me a blanket
with a picture of Wonder Woman and said:
"She is a very brave superhero, if you
need help, her power will fill
the blanket and it will protect you
from every monster in the world, because
it works like a shield and will not
let anyone hurt you."

Dad looked at mum and added:
"You know, when I was small, grandpa used
to apply this anti-monster ointment on me, it would
scare them away and I can tell you it really works.
Would you like me to bring it?"
"Yes, I really would" - I figured we have never
tried an anti-monster ointment before but why
not try, maybe grandpa's recipe really could help.
Not long after dad came back with
a round box – on the top you
could see a ghost with a large X on it."Dad, but
this is a ghost, not a monster" - I said.
"That is correct but it is just a symbol, the ointment
actually works on all boogeymen."
Then mum and dad started to put the ointment
on me in the most important
places, which are the hands and the feet, as monsters
always attack your limbs, this is what mum said.

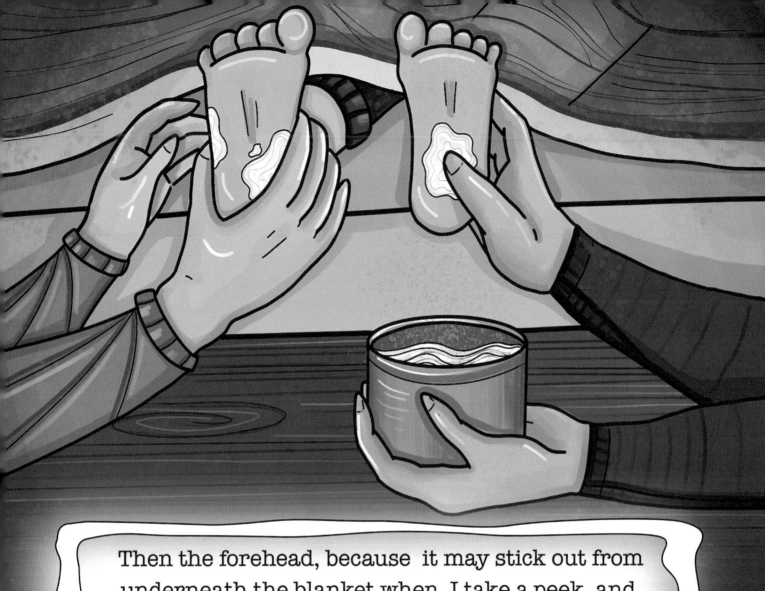

Then the forehead, because it may stick out from underneath the blanket when I take a peek, and that was it. It was quite pleasant and it smelled a bit familiar, kinda like mum's balm, but maybe it was supposed to smell this way, so that I would feel better.After all, my parents know what I need.

Dad said that he had one more idea, which
could banish the evil guest forever.
He said he would wait outside my room
with a specialghost - catcher, and if this
specimen reveals itself with all the bustle
and noise, I should call dad so that he
can come, catch it, and throw it out
of the window. And then it would all be over.
I did what he told me to do.

Something grunted, gurgled...
"Daddyyyyy!"

Dad came and got the Raven Stench
into the catcher with one move, and then
he ran out to the balcony.
"Nenia"- he called, walking
towards me - "It is done,
I got rid of it once and for all.
Now you can sleep sound, nothing
and nobody will bother you now.
Sweet dreams, my princess."

I got one more kiss from each parent
and I don't even
remember when I fell asleep.
And I now think to myself that it
is really cool to have such
a Great Guy as my dad, for me
he is a real hero.
Because who else but my
dad would get rid of
the monsters with
such cleverness!

The first story titled "Nenia vs the Night Monsters"

from series "The Adventures of Little Nenia"

I dedicate myself to an exceptional girl, thanks to whom

I am the best version of myself.

Honey, you are my greatest creation.

For my daughter - Hanna

Mum.

Thank you for purchase.

Visit us on:

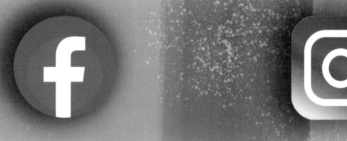

and enter

"The World of Nenia".

 Author – **Maria Piórkowska-Urbaniak**

 Illustrations – **Kaja Borzdyńska**

 Graphic design – **Paweł Urbaniak**

 Translation into English – **Marta Jesswein**

Contact – **pawelurbaniak.eu@gmail.com**

+48 691 624 114

Printed in Great Britain
by Amazon